Five years ago in the village of Berk, dragons and Vikings were enemies. But with Hiccup's help, everyone now lived in peace. And the Vikings had discovered a new favourite hobby: dragon racing!

Hiccup skipped the day's race to explore with Toothless. Now that Vikings could ride dragons, a whole new world awaited them.

After blasting through the finish line, Astrid and her dragon, Stormfly, flew off to find Hiccup. He was adding new discoveries to his map, and asked her where she had been.

"Winning races," she replied. "Where have you been?"

"Avoiding my dad," he said. "He asked me to be chief, but I want to explore—to figure out where I belong."

Astrid and Hiccup flew off with their dragons and discovered a new land covered in icy ruins.

That's when a dragon trapper named Eret captured Stormfly in his net. He said he was capturing dragons for a man named Drago to use in his dragon army.

With Toothless's help, Stormfly escaped.

"You will never hold on to those dragons," Eret yelled after them.

"Drago will come for them all!"

Hiccup raced back to Berk and warned Stoick about Drago and his dragon army.

Stoick's eyes were wide. "Drago Bludvist is a madman!"

"You know him?" Hiccup was surprised.

"Yes, and if he has built a dragon army, we must prepare for war!" Stoick replied.

"But it's our duty to keep the peace," Hiccup protested. "Let's follow the trappers and find Drago so we can talk some sense into him."

"Peace is over, Hiccup," Stoick replied. "We have to protect Berk. No one sets foot off this island until I give the word. Lower the doors!"

Hiccup, Toothless, Astrid, and Stormfly flew through the storm doors just before they closed. They went looking for Eret, but Eret found them first.

"Net 'em, lads!" he yelled to his crew.

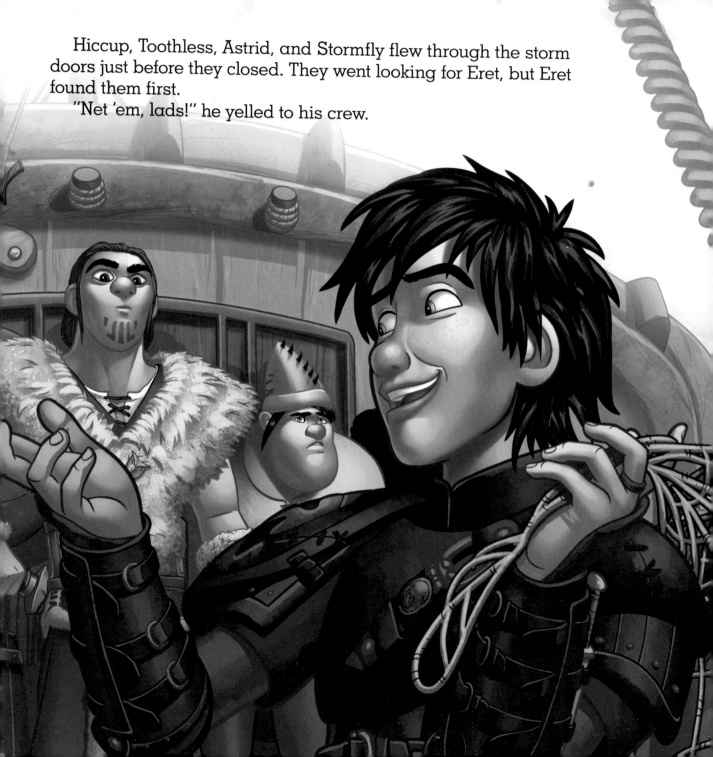

But Hiccup and Astrid surrendered.

"I want to change Drago's mind about dragons," Hiccup explained to Eret. "And yours, too. Right here, right now."

Before he could do anything, Snotlout, Stoick, Gobber, Ruffnut, Tuffnut, and the others came to rescue Astrid, Hiccup, and their dragons.

But Hiccup refused to be rescued. "If I could change your mind about dragons," he told Stoick as he flew away on Toothless, "I can change Drago's mind, too."

Stoick and Gobber went after him, telling Astrid and the others to return to Berk.

Hiccup and Toothless were flying in the cold air when suddenly a masked dragon rider appeared and began circling them. Another dragon came at them from behind, tearing Hiccup off of his saddle, and sending Toothless plummeting into the icy water.

"Hey! You left my dragon back there!" Hiccup yelled at the dragon rider. But the masked rider said nothing and motioned for the other dragon to follow, with Hiccup in its claws.

When they landed in a chamber inside a large mountain, the dragon rider stared at Hiccup's face.

"Hiccup?" the dragon rider whispered. "Could it be?" The rider removed the mask and Hiccup was surprised to see a woman's face.

"Should I know you?" Hiccup asked.

"No. You were only a babe," she answered softly. "But a mother never forgets."

Hiccup was shocked. "You're my mother?" he cried. "I have questions! Where have you been all this time? What have you been doing?"

Valka motioned for Hiccup to follow her. She led him to an enormous oasis filled with thousands of kinds of dragons.

Hiccup looked around in awe. He suddenly understood. "You've been rescuing dragons," Hiccup said.

Valka nodded. "This is the home of the great Bewilderbeast, the king of all dragons. This is a safe haven for dragons everywhere."

Meanwhile, Astrid became worried when Stoick and Gobber still had not returned with Hiccup and Toothless.

"We have to find them!" she told Ruffnut, Tuffnut, Snotlout, and the others.

Together, they captured Eret and forced him to lead them to Drago, thinking that Hiccup would be there.

When they arrived on Drago's ship, Eret announced, "Drago, always great to see you, my friend! Well, as you can see, I'm right on time with a new batch of dragons, just like I promised. I also caught you their riders, no extra charge. Turns out there's a whole bunch of them out there."

Drago was outraged. "How many dragon riders?" he roared.

"Just a few," Eret said. "They won't know where you're hiding, I promise you that."

"Oh, yes they will!" Astrid shouted. "We have tracking dragons."

Drago was furious. "First there was one rider. Now all of Berk." He glared at Eret. "And you led them to me!" Drago decided to attack Dragon Mountain immediately.

Back on the mountain, Valka didn't believe Hiccup when he said that dragons and Vikings were living in peace, and asked Hiccup to help her rescue Berk's dragons.

"Drago is coming for them all," Valka said.

"He's coming for yours too," Hiccup replied. "Let's go talk to him together."

But Valka refused to talk to Drago. Hiccup was about to leave to find Drago on his own when Stoick arrived.

"Dad, there's something you need to know," Hiccup said. "Unlike most surprises I spring on you, this is one you'll like."

Stoick looked up and gasped as though he was seeing a ghost. Valka stood before him.

Valka took a deep breath. "I know what you're going to say. How could I have stayed away all of these years?"

To her surprise, Stoick drew her close. "Will you come home, Val? Will you be my wife again?"

Their tender moment was interrupted by a loud boom. On the beach below, Drago was launching his attack with catapults.

"We have to save the dragons!" Valka yelled before rushing out.

Her dragons flew down to the beach, picking up Drago's soldiers and

"Whatever happens, keep hitting the mountain! Ready the traps!" Drago yelled to his soldiers.

Drago began using his dragons as bait. When Valka's dragons tried to rescue the dragons inside Drago's giant metal traps, the jaws of the trap closed around them. Drago was very determined, and he was winning.

Hiccup tried to reason with Drago, but he refused to listen.
Valka confronted Drago on the beach, bringing out the Bewilderbeast.
"You cannot control our dragons!" she told Drago, "because they are
controlled by the alpha."
"Then it's a good thing I brought a challenger," Drago replied.

A second, huge Bewilderbeast rose from the lagoon! Drago ordered his Bewilderbeast to attack Valka's. Their fight ended with a final swipe that took Valka's Bewilderbeast down.

All of the dragons in the land—even Toothless—bowed their heads, acknowledging their new alpha dragon, before following him and Drago to Berk.

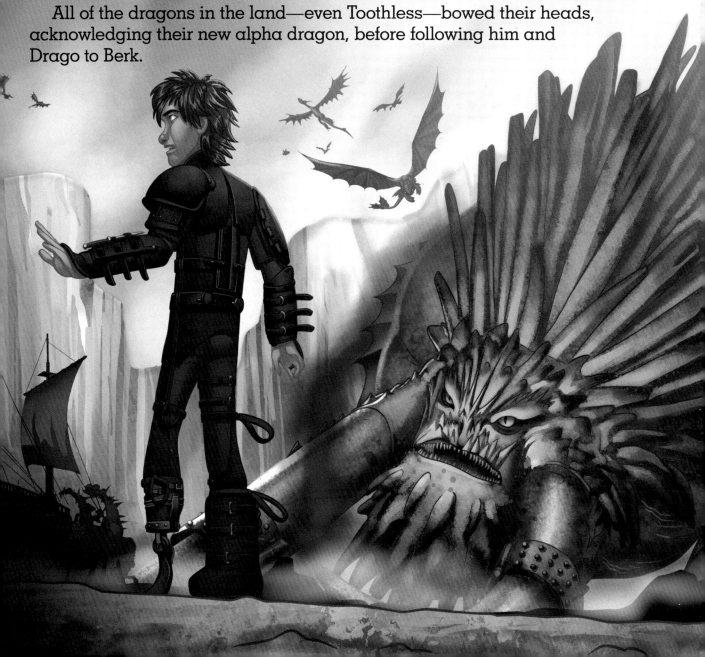

With no dragons left to fly, Hiccup realized there was no way to get home. Then he had an idea: the hatchlings.

"They're babies. They won't listen to anyone," Hiccup said. He remembered Valka had told him they wouldn't even obey the Bewilderbeast.

Hiccup and the others climbed on the backs of the dragon hatchlings and rode them back to Berk.

When they arrived, Berk was covered in ice. Drago's army had already led most of the dragons away, but Drago still had Toothless with him.

Hiccup was convinced he could break the Bewilderbeast's control over Toothless. Atop a hatchling, Hiccup approached Drago and Toothless.

"You'd never hurt me," Hiccup said to Toothless soothingly. "You are my best friend, bud. My best friend. I won't leave you. I won't let you go."

It worked! Hiccup's voice broke the spell. Together, Hiccup and Toothless fought Drago and the Bewilderbeast until both retreated.

With Drago and his Bewilderbeast gone, Toothless became the new alpha dragon, and Hiccup had accepted the role of chief.

With Toothless at his side, Hiccup knew he had nothing to fear. He knew the other side would have armies and armadas.

But the people of Berk would have their dragons.